APRIL

MAY

JUNE

OCTOBER

NOVEMBER

DECEMBER

£4.99

Printed and Published in Great Britain by D. C. THOMSON & CO., LTD.,
185 Fleet Street, London, EC4A 2HS.
© D. C. THOMSON & CO., LTD., 1997 ISBN 0-85116-617-2

OLIVER TWISTER

BAH! IT'S A MISERABLE LIFE BEING AN EVIL OLD ROGUE. WHEEZE!

ICY DRAUGHT!

WHEEZE! THAT'S IT! I'VE JUST HAD A WIZARD WHEEZE!

PYOING!

Later —

WONDER WHERE EVERYONE'S GOING WITH ALL THESE ANTYKES, TEEK.

I THINK HE MEANS ANTIQUES, TYKE.

SO THAT'S IT!

ROGUE'S GALLERY ANTIQUE SHOPPE. Best prices paid!

Inside —

THIS WAS MY FATHER'S. I'M TOLD IT PLAYS BEAUTIFULLY.

GIVES IT 'ERE THEN.

M-MY MING VASE!

SCREECH! HOWL! SCRAPE!

MY GOODNESS!

TINKLE!

From the DANDY BANK

SILLY STATEMENTS

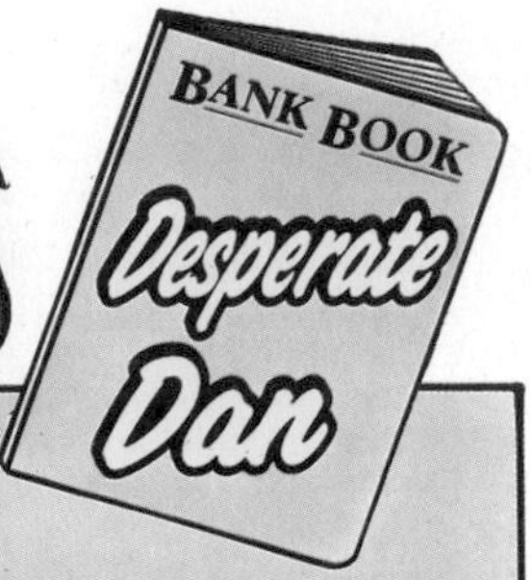

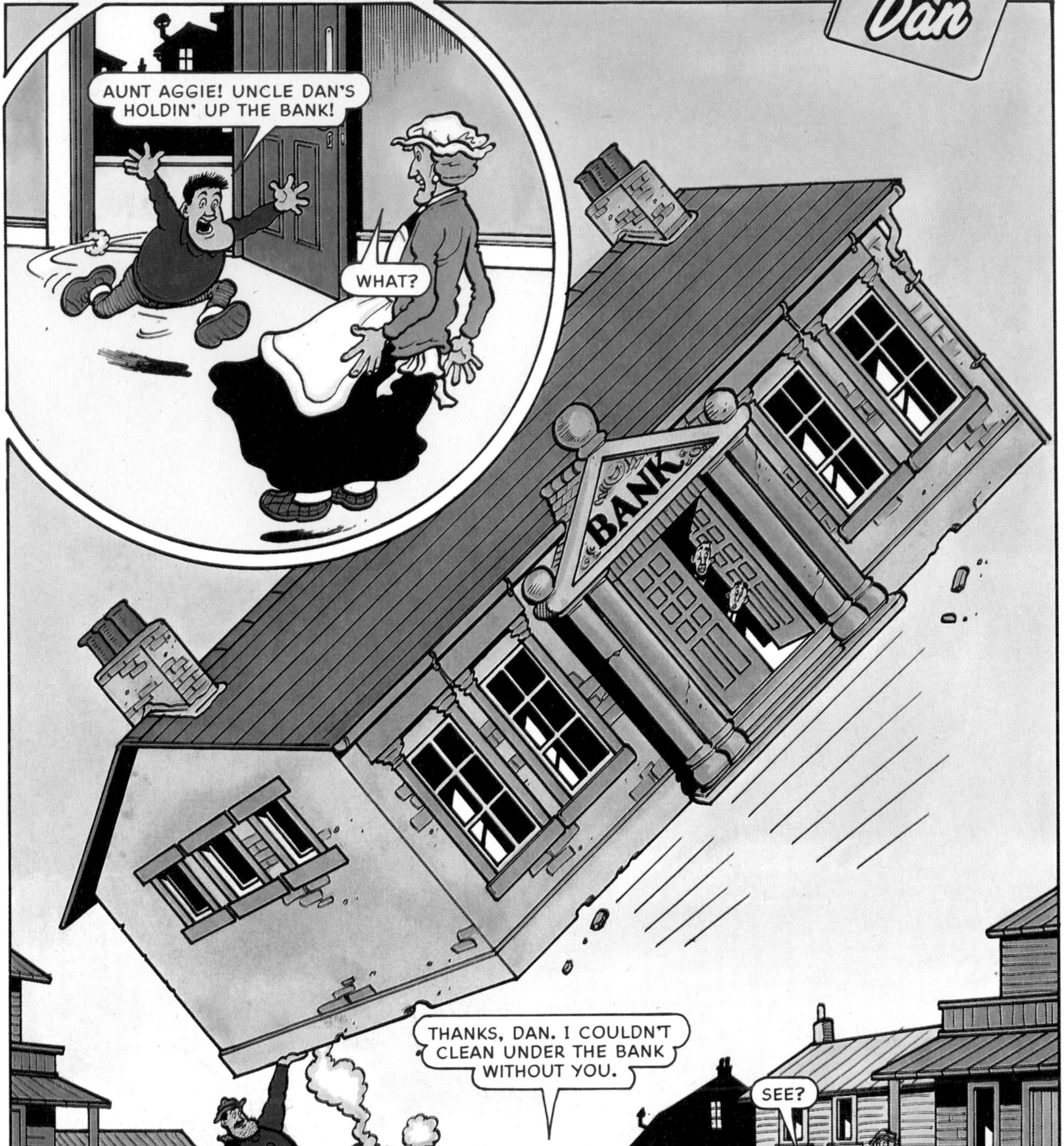

KORKY'S ALPHAKIT

A LARM

B IRDWATCHING

WOOF!

C ATTERY

WANTED
A FISHCAKE
WITH A
FILE IN IT.

D ARTS

THUNK!

E TCHING

SCRAPE! SCRIBBLE!

F ISHING

FRESH FISH

INDOORS

STUCK

JIG·SAW

KITS

NERVOUS

VET WAITING ROOM

OVER CURIOUS

SCRATCHING POST

SCRITCH!
SCRATCH
RIP!
SCRATCH!

TERROR

DOG POUND

WOOF!

BLINKY.

OH, WHAT EXCITEMENT.

I'M GETTING A PUPPY FROM THE DOGS' HOME.

DOGS HOME

SPACE CENTRE

THIS MUST BE THE EXERCISE YARD.

Meanwhile, in the space centre —

IS BLINKTOWN BOBBY READY, DOCTOR COMET?

IGNITION
LIFT OFF
TEA
COFFEE

AS READY AS A PUPPY CAN BE FOR HIS FIRST TRIP INTO SPACE, DOCTOR MOON.

50P

OUT, YA LITTLE VARMINT!

BOOT!

OWOO!

SKID!

WHUMP!

YEESH!

DRAT! THE LAW.

HALLO AGAIN, LITTLE PARDNER.

HAVING FUN PLAYING?

PAT PAT!

SQUISH

SHOV

UH? BIG GALOOT! YOU'VE JAMMED MAH HAT OVER MAH EYES.

TOTTER

AH CAN'T SEE!

GLUB!

SPLOOSH!

THAT JUST PLUMB RATTLE-SNAKIN' DOES IT!

DRIP

One day —

And then —

GLOOMPH!

I SAY! GET OUT OF MY PUMPKIN, LORD BLITHERING.

Next —

GLUG-GLUG!

SPLOP!

YIKES! TIME I HOPPED IT.

BATTEN DOWN THE HATCHES. LOAD THE TORPEDOES!

AYE-AYE, COLONEL.

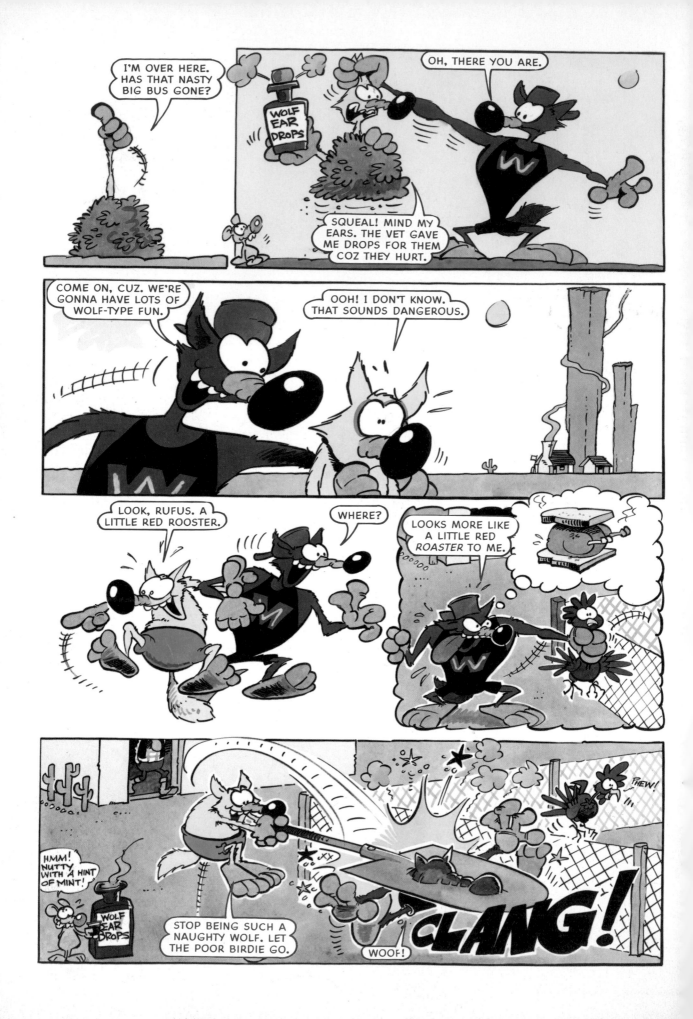

Dragon Trail

The year is 997 A.D. — the middle of the Dark Ages. A time when people still believed in magic . . . . . . and monsters.

GRANDMOTHER, LOOK! A FALLING STAR!

IT IS AN OMEN. BAD THINGS ARE COMING.

AWAY FROM THE WINDOW, ROBBIE. BACK TO YOUR LESSON, CHILD.

". . . AND FOR THE KING'S MEN TO PROVE THEIR LOYALTY, THEY SLEW THE MIGHTY DRAGONS!"

HAVE YOU EVER SEEN A DRAGON, GRANDMOTHER?

WHEN I WAS YOUNG. BEFORE THEY WERE ALL HUNTED DOWN.

I WOULD LOVE TO BE A KNIGHT AND FIGHT A DRAGON.

YES, AND SO WOULD MOST BOYS. NOW, OFF TO BED WITH YOU.

AYE. IT'S AN OMEN. THERE ARE DARK DAYS AHEAD OF US.

The woods had never been explored and for some the going was tough.

NO TIME TO REST, LAD. WE CAN'T AFFORD TO LOSE THOSE SUPPLIES.

COMING, SEPTIMUS.

HISSSSSS

WHAT WAS THAT?

NOTHING . . . YOUR IMAGINATION.

SEE? THE MARK OF THE DRAGON! WE MUST BE CLOSE!

But further on.

WE CAMP HERE FOR THE NIGHT.

VERY WELL. WE SHALL SCOUT ON AHEAD.

As night grows darker, a figure slips out of camp.

I WONDER IF THE STRANGERS HAVE FOUND ANYTHING.

WHY HAVE THEY CAMPED OVER HERE?

IT'S COLD, TORL. GET US A FIRE.

ONLY GOOD FOR LIGHTING FIRES! NO USE AGAINST THAT . . . CREATURE!

STUPID LASERS!

MAGIC!?

THEY DID THEIR JOB, DIDN'T THEY? BURNT THAT ILLAGE TO A CRISP.

YEAH. NOW WE CAN USE THOSE IGNORANT SAVAGES TO KILL THE CREATURE WHILE WE STEAL THE SHIP!

SHIP? BUT WE'RE MILES FROM THE SEA. WHAT ARE THEY . . . ?

THEN THE WHOLE GALAXY IS OURS TO ROB!

ROBBERS? I MUST WARN . . . OH!

CRACK!

GRAHAM·P·MANLEY·'95

WHAT IN . . .?!

ROBBIE!?

DON'T KILL IT! IT'S NOT EVIL!

GET THAT BRAT!

AAAGHH!!

THUNK!

THE STRANGERS DESTROYED CAIRNTOWN WITH THOSE WEAPONS!

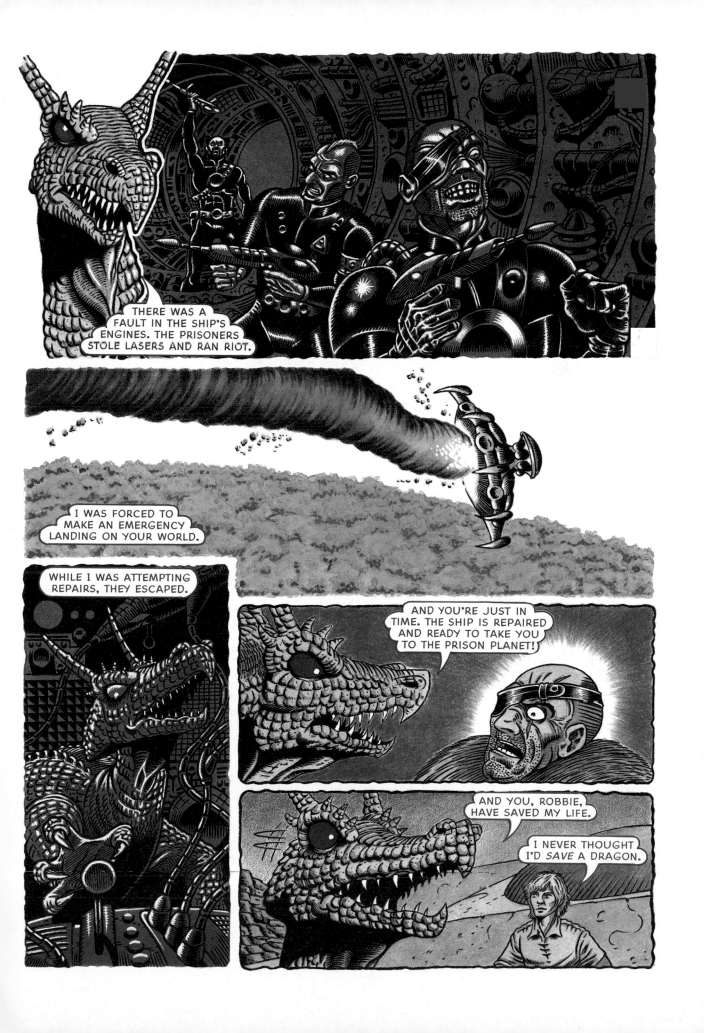

F

Soon —

IT'S A NICE DAY FOR A DRIVE. MUNCH! CHOMP!

CRASH!

OOPS! FANCY BUMPING INTO YOU, CHIEFY.

POLICE

GRR!

YOU'VE WON A MEAL FOR ONE IDIOT IN THE POLICE RAFFLE. HERE!

BOP! WOP!

OW! OUCH! I'M TOUCHED!

THIS IS THE RESTAURANT BUT I'M PUZZLED. I DIDN'T BUY A TICKET.

YE BATTER

Inside —

MONSEWER BLUEBONCE. WELCOME. I WEEL SHOW YOU ZE KITCHEN.

OOH! THAT'LL BE NICE.

Can Bananaman get out of this tricky situation? See Page 129.

GROWING PAYNES

Then —

PLOP!

HOWL! I KNOW WHAT I'LL NEED SOON . . .

Back home —

. . . A DOCTOR! ACHOO! SNUFFLE!

THIS IS ALL YOUR FAULT — GIVING MY PETAL A CHILL! YOU NEED YOUR HEAD EXAMINED!

TISSUES

From the DANDY BANK
SILLY STATEMENTS

NOW WHERE'S SHE GONE?

I ALWAYS THOUGHT IT WAS A WIG.

LIFT

GRRR!

AHA! *THERE* YOU ARE!

NABBED.

KEEP YOUR HAIR ON.

PLONK

EEK!

AND OUR TRIP IS TO THE SWEET FACTORY.

EH?

WOT?

SWEETS?

GANGWAY!

COME ON. HURRY UP, MISS. NO SLOUCHING.

EEKS!

ZOOM!

FACTORY FLOOR

SIGH! WHAT A SLOBBERICIOUS WHIFF!

THIS MACHINE SQUIRTS FONDANT ICING ONTO THESE TOFFEE BARS.

TIME TO GET NAUGHTY, WILF.

DROOL!

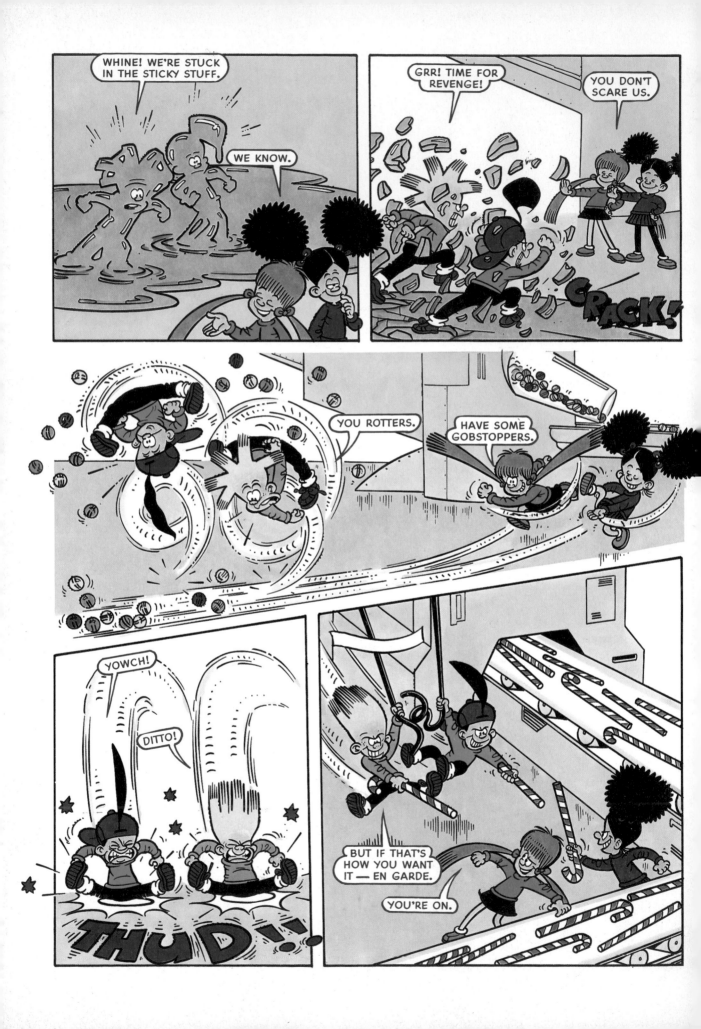

BANANAMAN
PART 2

Bananaman has gone into hiding and Doctor Gloom and his crooked pals are running riot. A wave of crime sweeps the country.

And —

I WAS RIGHT. I'M GONNA GET THAT REWARD. I'LL BE RICH.

SIGH! I HOPE I FIND SOMETHING TO EAT IN HERE.

AARGH!

Soon —

HOI! WHAT'S THAT GARBAGE DOING IN HERE?

THAT'S NO WAY TO TALK ABOUT A LAW-ABIDING TRAMP, CHIEF.

LOOK! THAT'S HIM!

WANTED
ALIVE or DAFT

OH, REALLY?

O'REILLY! IT REALLY IS.

Bananaman tells his story. SOB! SOB! AND I'LL NEVER BE A CRIME-FIGHTING HERO AGAIN. SOB!

OOH! WHAT A SOB STORY.

THE WORRY IS DRIVING ME UP THE WALL. SEE?

THAT'S THE ANSWER. YOU CAN EAVESDROP ON GLOOM'S HEADQUARTERS.

So —

HM! NOW WHERE IS GLOOM HIDING? LET ME SEE.

GLOOM'S HIDE-OUT!

YOU ARE HERE

That night —

THIS IS THE PLACE. I'LL BET GLOOM'S UP TO NO GOOD.

WE'LL GO FOR THE ROYAL MINT NEXT.

HEE-HEE!

Suddenly —

I KNEW THE DANDY READERS WOULDN'T SWALLOW THAT. I'M BACK — HANDSOME AS EVER, EH?

SCHLOOP!

THAT BANANA-FLAVOURED CUSTARD MADE ME NORMAL AGAIN.

IT'S HIM — TWICE AS LARGE AS LIFE.

TAKE THAT!

AND THAT!

GOOD GROUPING, FRIENDS. BUT USELESS!

OOFYAH!

CRUNCH!

Later —

I TOLD YOU SWEETS WERE BAD FOR YOU, ERIC.

YES, MUM.

WHAT DO *YOU* THINK, READERS?

From the DANDY BANK
SILLY STATEMENTS
BANK BOOK
The Dandy
I WANT MY MONEY NOW!
YOU STILL HAVE 6 HADDOCK AND 4 COD IN YOUR ACCOUNT.
BANK BOOK
KORKY
SLOBBER!
OOCH!
CRASH!

JANUARY

FEBRUARY

MARCH

JULY

AUGUST

SEPTEMBER